Jeremy Strong once worked in a bakery, putting the jam into three thousand doughnuts every night. Now he puts the jam in stories instead, which he finds much more exciting. At the age of three, he fell out of a first-floor bedroom window and landed on his head. His mother says that this damaged him for the rest of his life and refuses to take any responsibility. He loves writing stories because he says it is 'the only time you alone have complete control and can make anything happen'. His ambition is to make you laugh (or at least snuffle). Jeremy Strong lives near Bath with four cats and a flying cow.

Jeremy Strong

Pandemonium at School

For Jane: A great friend and a brilliant teacher, without whom this story could never have existed.

PUFFIN BOOKS

Published by the Penguin Group
Penguin Books Ltd, 80 Strand, London WC2R 0RL, England
Penguin Putnam Inc., 375 Hudson Street, New York, New York 10014, USA
Penguin Books Australia Ltd, 250 Camberwell Road, Camberwell, Victoria 3124, Australia
Penguin Books Canada Ltd, 10 Alcorn Avenue, Toronto, Ontario, Canada M4V 3B2
Penguin Books India (P) Ltd, 11 Community Centre, Panchsheel Park, New Delhi – 110 017, India
Penguin Books (NZ) Ltd, Cnr Rosedale and Airborne Roads, Albany, Auckland, New Zealand
Penguin Books (South Africa) (Pty) Ltd, 24 Sturdee Avenue, Rosebank 2196, South Africa

Penguin Books Ltd, Registered Offices: 80 Strand, London WC2R 0RL, England

www.penguin.com

First published by A & C Black (Publishers) Limited 1990
Published in Puffin Books 1999
19

Text copyright © Jeremy Strong, 1990
Illustrations copyright © Judy Brown, 1990
All rights reserved

The moral right of the author and illustrator has been asserted

Typeset in Monotype Baskerville

Made and printed in England by Clays Ltd, St Ives plc

British Library Cataloguing in Publication Data
A CIP catalogue record for this book is available from the British Library

ISBN-13: 978–0–14–130495–3

www.greenpenguin.co.uk

Mixed Sources
Product group from well-managed
forests and other controlled sources
www.fsc.org Cert no. SA-COC-1592
© 1996 Forest Stewardship Council

Penguin Books is committed to a sustainable future
for our business, our readers and our planet.
The book in your hands is made from paper
certified by the Forest Stewardship Council.

Contents

1 The New Teacher

There was a long, long silence during which time Mr Shrapnell stared dully at the telephone still dangling in his left hand. Slowly he raised his eyes until they met those of Mrs Bunt, the school secretary. She put a thin hand to her mouth, already anxious.

'Oh, Mr Shrapnell, what is the matter? Who was that on the phone?'

For the first time the Headmaster seemed to become aware of the machine that had brought the bad news. He carefully replaced it on the receiver and raised his eyes to Mrs Bunt again, spearing her with a steel-grey glare. 'That was Mr David, Mrs Bunt. He went sleepwalking last night, fell downstairs and broke his arm and two ribs.'

'Oh the poor man. The poor, poor man!' cried Mrs Bunt, not even noticing that the Headteacher had clamped his jaws together and seemed to be grinding his teeth with grim fury. Mrs Bunt had now clasped both hands in an attitude of deep prayer. 'The poor man. What he must be suffering, and him with his bad back too.'

Mr Shrapnell could take no more. He sprang to his feet and strode round his desk. 'I don't care how many broken legs or bad backs he's got, Mrs Bunt! I don't care if he's been sawn in half, stuffed with green peppers and eaten by gourmet cannibals from the depths of Borneo. I don't care, I don't care – as long as he arrives every day by ten minutes to nine and teaches his class of thirty-two nine year olds. That is his job, Mrs Bunt, do you understand?'

The secretary really was trembling now.
It was at times like these that she
wondered why she continued to work for
Mr Shrapnell. His rages were so
unpredictable. It was like walking blindfold
across a minefield. It was also at times like
these she remembered children with cut
knees, grazed elbows and scratches in the
most unexpected places. Then there were
the lumps and bumps she had smoothed

and the tears she had wiped dry, and she knew why she carried on working at Dullandon Primary School.

Mr Shrapnell leaned towards her, his right eye beginning to twitch in one corner. He glared over her shoulder to the wall behind and stabbed at it with a thick finger.

'Do you see that, Mrs Bunt? It's the school timetable. That is what the school works to. Look, look! Monday, May the third. There it is – see? There!'

The secretary nodded quickly as Mr Shrapnell almost pushed her face into the timetable. 'And see here, this is Mr David's class on Monday, May the third. Maths, English, History and then –' the Headteacher lowered his voice to a grave whisper – 'Science, Mrs Bunt, Science.' For a moment he was lost in thought, then he turned back to the secretary. 'Now, tell me, Mrs Bunt, who is going to teach Mr David's class today? Or tomorrow? Or the day after that? He will be away from school for at least a week. It's a disaster!' The Head gave a shudder at the thought of such selfishness on the part of the injured Mr David.

The school secretary calmed herself. 'I'll get on the phone at once Mr Shrapnell. I'm sure we can find a replacement for poor Mr David.'

'And stop calling him poor!' yelled the Head, as she hurried back to her office. 'He's going to destroy the running of the school. I've spent months perfecting that timetable!' She heard his door slam shut and sat down on her chair with relief.

'One day,' she promised herself, 'I am going to tell Mr Shrapnell just what I think of him. Now, let's try Mrs Perkins. She's filled in for us before.' But there was no reply from Mrs Perkins. 'Well how about Miss Juniper?'

This time there was an answer, but when Miss Juniper heard that Dullandon Primary School was a teacher short she almost spat down the phone. 'You can tell Mr Shrapnell to go and boil his head,' she told Mrs Bunt. 'I'll not work for that old ratbag again!'

'I know just how you feel,' murmured Mrs Bunt as she dialled Mr Dunwoody's number. But Mr Dunwoody had retired from teaching altogether. Mrs Bunt tried four more supply teachers but they all had an excuse or they were out. Mrs Bunt began to get the impression that nobody wanted to come near the school and she had almost run out of names on her list.

The door was suddenly flung open and Mr Shrapnell's angry head appeared. 'Have you got someone yet, Mrs Bunt? School starts in ten minutes.'

'I'm afraid Mrs Perkins can't come, Miss Juniper is, er, otherwise engaged, Mr Dunwoody has –'

'Don't give me feeble excuses, woman. This is an emergency. Find me a teacher for Mr David's class.' The door slammed shut whipping a pile of papers from Mrs Bunt's desk and scattering them across the carpet.

The secretary got down on her hands and knees and searched for the list of supply teachers. At last it was found, beneath the caretaker's order for six tons of lavatory cleaner. Mrs Bunt groaned. 'I do wish the caretaker would spell things properly.' She crossed out the 'o' in tons and changed it to six tins. 'I should think six tons would last us about a hundred years. Now, who's left on this list – Mrs Green and Miss Pandemonium.'

The secretary picked up the phone again. There was no answer from Mrs Green and that left Miss Pandemonium. The phone had hardly rung once before it was answered at the other end by a very excited voice.

'Don't you worry,' gabbled Miss Pandemonium. 'I shall be over in a jiffy. No – even quicker than that – in a jiff! I'll grab my bag and dash upstairs and put on some make-up – no I won't – I'll do that in the van on the way over. My goodness, school starts in five minutes. I shall have to get a move on.'

'Miss Pandemonium,' began Mrs Bunt. 'Do you know the –'

'Dunderbank School, isn't it?' shouted Miss Pandemonium down the telephone. Her voice came over in a very odd way because she was hopping about on one foot while she was talking, trying to pull on one half of a pair of tights.

'Are you all right?' Mrs Bunt inquired anxiously, as a huge crash rolled down the telephone line and fell into her right ear.

'Fine! Fine!' Miss Pandemonium's voice sounded a bit distant. This was probably because she had fallen one way and the telephone had whizzed off in the opposite direction. 'Don't worry, I'm on my way,' announced Miss Pandemonium, and the phone went dead before Mrs Bunt had time to tell her that the school was called Dullandon, not Dunderbank.

Mrs Bunt gave her head a little shake as if to get some sense back into it. She rose from her seat to go and tell the Headmaster, then paused for a second. A tiny smile found its way on to her thin lips. She had a feeling about Miss Pandemonium, the sort of feeling that made her feel nervous and just a bit giggly. Heaven alone knew why she should feel like that. Perhaps it was the thought of Mr Shrapnell meeting the new teacher.

Anyhow, the Head was delighted to hear the news. He glanced at his watch. 'Four, no, three minutes to go before the whistle for the start of school. Well done, Mrs Bunt. Let's hope she can get here in time. What do we know about her?'

Mrs Bunt glanced at the list of supply teachers. 'She says here that she will teach anything to anyone.'

The Head rubbed his hands together. 'Indeed? Good, good. I hope she gets a

move on. I must go and blow the whistle.'
He grabbed a whistle from the back of his
door and strode across the hall to the
playground.

The children were screaming and
shouting and dashing round like the balls
in a pinball machine. But the children
meant little to Mr Shrapnell. He ran the
school like his own private army. There
was a place for everything, and everything
in its place. There was a time for
everything, and everything . . . his eyes
were on his watch. Ten seconds, nine,
eight – the whistle was in his mouth at the
ready.

A piercing shrill brought the rush and
dash and noise to a halt. Every child stood
stock still, frozen to the spot. 'Frazer! Your
foot moved. Stand still, boy! That girl
there, yes you, stop scratching!'

Mr Shrapnell glanced across to the car park. Still no sign of Miss Pandemonium. From the distance came the faint sound of a siren. Probably a fire engine, he noted mentally. He began to call out the names of classes. Lines of children filed silently into school. The siren came closer. Some children turned to see if it would pass by the school gates. Would it be a fire engine or a police car?

There was a screech of tyres at the corner of the road and an ambulance veered into view. Lights were flashing and the siren wee-wahed furiously. It whizzed past the school while everyone stared. Not even Mr Shrapnell could resist the thrill.

The ambulance suddenly screeched to a halt and reversed, its siren still screaming. A side window flew open and an arm shot out, making a grand signal for a right turn.

Then the ambulance growled, scrunged its gears, leaped forward down the school drive and skidded to a halt in the car park.

A short figure jumped out, pulling six assorted bags after her and spilling half of them on to the tarmac. She gazed around for a moment and ran a hand through a head of hair that looked like a rook's nest. She had lipstick halfway up one cheek and eyeshadow over most of her nose. She gave Mr Shrapnell a cheery grin and staggered across the playground towards him, trailing bags behind.

'Morning!' she cried. 'What a lovely morning too – Violet Pandemonium – how do you do?'

'But, but,' began Mr Shrapnell. 'That ambulance –'

'Smashing isn't it? I bought it at a car

auction last year. Everything still works you know, siren, lights, the lot!'

'I heard,' muttered Mr Shrapnell.

'Shall we go in? No time to waste,' said Miss Pandemonium. 'Lead on, Macduff – that's Shakespeare you know.'

Mr Shrapnell gave a low groan and

trailed behind Miss Pandemonium into the
school, picking up all the bits she dropped
as she went.

2 The Great Dart Contest

'This is Class Three,' said Mr Shrapnell. Thirty-two children sat silent and still, staring first at their new teacher, then at Mr Shrapnell, and finally, irresistibly back at the new teacher. 'Class Three, this is Miss Pandemonium.'

Violet Pandemonium gave the class a big smile and dropped another two of her bags. 'Good morning, everyone!' she sang and immediately disappeared beneath the tables to pick up her belongings.

'Good Mor-ning Miss-Pan-dee-moh-nee-umm,' chanted Class Three, even though she had vanished from their sight.

'Mr David is ill,' grunted Mr Shrapnell. 'However, I am sure you are in good hands with Miss Pandemonium here. Oh, by the way, Miss Pandemonium, the timetable is pinned to the wall there. I think Maths comes first.'

'What's that?' came a faint voice from somewhere beneath the tables. 'Oooh, I've found a rubber that looks like an elephant. Anyone lost an elephant?' A hand appeared above the desk-tops waving a little pink rubber. 'Who's lost an elephant?'

Mr Shrapnell stared at the creature and the arm quite speechless. He had never

heard anything like it. As for Class Three, they were dumbstruck too. They waited breathlessly, expecting Mr Shrapnell to explode at any moment. But he didn't. He just stared at the thin hand waving the rubber elephant. Then Miss Pandemonium's face appeared as she clambered back to her feet. 'Come on, it must belong to someone,' she said brightly. 'Poor little elephant without a home.'

There was a faint snigger from the back of the class. Mr Shrapnell whirled round and glared into the depths of the classroom. He drew in his breath sharply. 'I shall leave you to it, Miss Pandemonium, and don't forget – Maths!'

Mr Shrapnell strode to the door and disappeared. There was a sigh of relief and the children slumped back in their chairs. Violet Pandemonium looked at them carefully. They gazed back at her with a dull expression in their eyes. Three of them were already looking in their desks.

'What are you doing?' asked Miss Pandemonium.

'Getting out our Maths books, miss.'

'Who said anything about Maths?' she asked gently. The three heads reappeared and eyed her carefully.

'We always do Maths on Monday,' said Rebecca.

'I see, well, we mustn't change the timetable, must we? Is this it over here?' Miss Pandemonium screwed up her eyes to read the vast sheet of paper which was covered with blue writing. There were lots of bits underlined with red. 'That does look interesting,' she said at last. 'Now then, Maths. Let's see, what's your name?'

'Peter, miss.'

'All right, Peter — what's two add two?'

Peter groaned with boredom. 'Four, miss.'

'Well done. And who are you?'

'Amy, miss.'

'Amy, what is six hundred and ninety-two, add five thousand two hundred and sixty, divided by eight?'

It was Amy's turn to groan. That was hopelessly hard to do in her head. 'Don't know, miss,' she whispered, and waited for a scream of anger.

'Neither do I,' smiled Miss Pandemonium. 'But it must be an awful lot. Well then, that's got our Maths done for the day. What do we do next?'

'It says English on the timetable, miss,' Amber called out.

'In that case please tell the class how to spell "cat".' Amber duly spelled the word.

'That's lovely,' said Miss Pandemonium.
'Now we've done our English. History
next, I believe. Anthony, when's your
birthday?'

'October the twenty-eighth, miss.'

Violet Pandemonium glanced at her
watch. 'Half-past nine and we've done the
whole timetable!'

'We haven't done Science yet,' groaned
Luke.

'We're always doing Science,' moaned
Wayne.

The classroom door burst open and Mr
Shrapnell poked his big head round the
frame. 'Everything all right, Miss
Pandemonium?' he snapped. 'Maths?'

'Doing it, Mr Shrapnell,' said Miss
Pandemonium cheerfully. For a moment
the two adults looked at each other. It
seemed as if Mr Shrapnell did not believe

her and she was waiting for him to say more. Meantime she just gazed at him steadily with her bright, grey eyes. Mr Shrapnell found the stare rather unnerving. He gave a curt nod, quietly pulled the door shut and went away.

Miss Pandemonium turned back to the class. 'Tell me what science you have done so far this term, Mark.'

'We've been doing a topic on birds, miss.'

'Have you? That sounds like fun.'

'We've done finches and ducks and gulls so far,' Mark went on, rather listlessly.

Miss Pandemonium now had her head buried deep inside one of her bags. 'If you carry on like that,' a muffled voice said from the bottom of the bag, 'you should have covered the whole bird kingdom in about two years' time. Ah, that's what I was after. Paul, give a sheet of this paper to everyone. Now, who can tell me what origami is?'

'Is she a pop star, miss?' asked Kerry.

'That's brilliant! What a wonderful name! Actually origami is a Japanese word and it means the art of folding paper. Paul's just given you a sheet of origami paper and I want you to fold it into a triangle, like this.'

Everyone busily folded their sheet. The door whizzed open. 'Maths?' inquired Mr Shrapnell, glaring suspiciously.

'Hold up your shapes, Class Three,' cried Miss Pandemonium. 'What are they?'

'Triangles!' shouted the class.

Mr Shrapnell frowned, growled, shut the door and went away. The children looked at each other and grinned. This was great.

'Now fold here. Bend that tip like so. Good, now squash the square section, turn it over and push in this angle here and there – you have a bird. Easy, wasn't it?'

There was a whisper of excitement as Class Three realized what they had just done, but Miss Pandemonium hadn't finished. 'Take the legs that are hanging down and pull gently – there!'

'Wow!' cried Karen. 'It flaps! It flaps its wings when you pull the legs!' Thirty-two origami birds were flapping about over the desktops. A rising chorus of bird calls began to fill the classroom. Miss Pandemonium joined in enthusiastically, climbing on to her desk and making her bird dive down.

'I'm a kestrel,' she cried. 'Keeaw! Keeeaw! Look out, John, you've just laid an egg!'

John smiled. 'Are you, sort of, well, mad, miss?' Violet stood up straight, thought for a moment and then jumped down.

'Quite possibly,' she told him. He smiled again.

'I thought you were,' he said happily.

'OK, birds down for a second,' Miss Pandemonium called. 'Who can tell me how birds fly?'

'Someone pulls their legs, miss!' shouted Wayne.

'I don't think so,' she laughed. She dug into her bag again and pulled out more origami paper. 'Make a paper dart that will go as far as possible,' said Miss Pandemonium.

Lee shifted uneasily. 'We're not allowed darts.'

'Has anyone told you not to make paper *aeroplanes*?'

'Only darts, miss,' grinned Jackie, hurriedly beginning to fold her paper into a supersonic mach-twelve aeroplane.

A few minutes later, darts were whizzing around the classroom and Miss Pandemonium called a halt. She took the class through to the hall where there was plenty of room, but throwing them across the hall was not good enough for Miss Pandemonium.

'We need more height. Pull those wall bars out. Seabirds launch themselves off clifftops, so the wall bars can be our cliff. That's it, smashing! Come on, everyone.'

Miss Pandemonium clambered up the side of the climbing frame and a host of children swarmed after her, clutching their darts.

'I always wanted to be a seabird when I was small,' said Violet. 'I wanted to be an

albatross. I wish I'd been born an
albatross.'

'Did you, miss?' Theresa looked at her
teacher quizzically. Miss Pandemonium
seemed ever so strange, but there was
something nice and comfortable about her
too. Theresa was prompted to say
something she had never told anyone. 'I've
always wanted to be a rabbit,' she
whispered.

'Oh, how lovely! And here we are. Right
everybody, one at a time – launch your
aeroplanes.'

One by one the children threw their

darts. Some did splendid nosedives straight into the hall floor. Some curved upwards at high speed and then slowly twirled round and round and down. Only two or three actually flew some distance, and as each throw took place it was carefully measured with a long tape.

Miss Pandemonium had made a dart of her own. It whizzed straight back over her shoulder and crashed into the wall behind. 'Oh dear, mine's gone backwards.' Class Three were laughing.

'Miss Pandemonium! What is all this noise?' Mr Shrapnell stood at the other end of the hall, glaring angrily at the floor which was covered with darts of all sizes. 'What on earth is going on here? Children, you know darts are NOT allowed.'

Miss Pandemonium grabbed a nearby rope and slid down to the bristling

Headteacher. 'Mr Shrapnell, we are making a serious investigation into the nature of flight. How can we do work on Birds without understanding the principle of flight? Look at my one. It's just flown backwards.' She thrust the dart into Mr Shrapnell's hands. 'Now, can you tell me why it went backwards? Watch.' She snatched it back, threw it, and once again it vanished over her shoulder. 'See? I told you so.'

Mr Shrapnell picked up the dart. He began to smooth one of the wings. 'I think it's because the . . .' He stopped suddenly and frowned angrily. 'Miss Pandemonium, this is not on the timetable and I don't think you should encourage children to –'

'This is Science, isn't it?' interrupted Violet, watching the Head with those bright, grey eyes again. 'I think Julie's dart has gone the furthest, so she's won. We'll go back to class and see if we can discover why her dart worked best. Would you like to come and help, Mr Shrapnell?'

The Head stepped back in horror and muttered something darkly about far too much work. Miss Pandemonium smiled and took the children back to class. As they went, Rebecca whispered to the others, 'I hope Miss P stays for ever and ever. She's brilliant!'

But Glenn was more thoughtful. 'She won't last long. You saw the way Shrapnoodle looked at her. He's going to get rid of her as soon as possible and then it will be back to the old boring ways. You wait and see.'

3 To Fly Like A Bird – Almost

'Miss Pandemonium,' began Mr Shrapnell, pacing back and forth behind his desk. 'You must understand the importance of rules. The children must do what you tell them to do.'

Violet smiled. 'That's why I'm so pleased, Mr Shrapnell. They're lovely children and they did exactly as I asked.'

Mr Shrapnell stopped pacing, stared at the ceiling as if it had just blown a raspberry at him, then turned to the new teacher. 'I beg your pardon, Miss Pandemonium?'

'Please, call me Violet. I was named after the flower you know. Mother always thought of me as a shrinking violet. I can't imagine why. I've always thought of myself as more like a dandelion, although of course that wouldn't sound quite right would it – Dandelion Pandemonium?'

'Miss Dandymonium!' yelled the Head. 'Please pay attention. Are you telling me you actually *asked* the children to make paper darts, climb the wall bars and fly them across the hall?'

'Yes, of course!'

'But there is nothing on the timetable about using the hall at that time. You were supposed to be doing English.' Miss Pandemonium gave the Head a curious glance. What a strange person he must be to let life be ruled by a timetable. 'You were supposed to be doing English. Instead, you asked the children to deliberately break the school rules and fly paper darts round the hall!'

'There wasn't enough room in class,' said Miss Pandemonium.

'You asked them to make paper darts! You might just as well have got them making helicopters or something equally stupid!'

Miss Pandemonium leaped to her feet. 'Helicopters! Mr Shrapnell, you are so clever. Here am I, sitting right in front of you and thinking what a silly old man you are, going on about paper darts, as if it mattered, and that silly old timetable too! And all the time you were thinking why waste time on darts when you could be making helicopters!'

'But Miss –' started Mr Shrapnell in horror. However, Violet Pandemonium was now in full flow, and not to be stopped.

'Of course it will be difficult. Making

the rotors won't be easy, and the flap angle will be vital. Oh Mr Shrapnell, you've opened my eyes. Why should we bother with silly old darts when we could really fly? We could really *fly*!' she repeated, and almost ran from the Headmaster's office.

Mr Shrapnell slumped back. He could not understand how she got away with it. Every time he pointed out what was wrong, it got twisted round until he didn't know what she would do or say next. What on earth was she up to now? He groaned loudly and buried his face in his hands.

Out in the secretary's office, Mrs Bunt heard the groan. She had caught all the conversation before as well. Now she was sitting in front of her typewriter and smiling quietly to herself. All her instincts

about Miss Pandemonium were proving
true, and Mrs Bunt was enjoying every
minute of it.

When the children returned to class after
lunch they found Miss Pandemonium up
to her knees in a pile of junk and looking
very excited. There were bits of balsa
wood and thin steel rods. There were

wheels, cogs, wires, batteries and bulbs. There were thin sticks, thick sticks and bits of string and tape.

Mr David's class stared at the jumble and whispered to each other. Miss Pandemonium suddenly stopped talking to herself and noticed the class for the first time. 'Ah! There you are! Afternoon, everyone.'

'Good Arf-ter-noon-Miss-Pan-dee –'

'Just call me Superwoman,' laughed Miss Pandemonium.

'Superwoman?' giggled Caroline.

'Yes, Superwoman, because this afternoon we are going to fly!'

'FLY!!' chorused Class Three.

'Exactly. Now, how many of you have a bicycle at school?'

Several hands went up. Violet counted and nodded at the same time. 'That's fine.

OK, if you've got a bicycle bring it over to the wall outside the classroom.'

Cheryl looked at her feet and began to mutter that bikes had to stay in the bike shed at all times. Miss Pandemonium ran a hand through her bird's nest of hair and fixed Cheryl with a twinkling pair of eyes. 'My dear, don't worry. Only a little while ago the Headmaster himself was telling me that children must do exactly as they are told. So, please fetch your bikes over to the wall there. Off you go.'

The children did not need to be told again and shortly there were nine bicycles propped up against the wall. They looked at them gravely. Kerry spoke up first.

'Please, miss, if we're going to fly, why do we need bikes?'

'Very good question, Kerry,' said Miss Pandemonium. 'Now I shall ask you one.

How does Man get himself into the air?'

'He jumps!' shouted Luke.

'Not quite the answer I expected but yes, he could jump. But how does he manage to stay up there if he wants to?'

'He goes in an aeroplane,' said John.

'Or a rocket, or a balloon,' Kelly added.

'Or a helicopter,' murmured Paul.

'Exactly,' nodded Miss Pandemonium.

'He doesn't usually go on a bicycle,' Rebecca pointed out.

'That is where you are quite wrong. What we are going to do is turn those bicycles into helicopters. You will climb on board, pedal quickly and the helicopter rotor blades will turn round and up you will go.' Miss Pandemonium spoke so confidently she could have persuaded a bumblebee that it could fly to Mars.

There was a moment's silence. The

whole class looked through the window at the ordinary everyday bicycles leaning against the wall. All at once they gave a yell of delight and dived into the pile of bits and pieces at Miss Pandemonium's feet, while she called out helpful bits of advice.

A great noise of hammering and sawing began. Some children got huge sheets of paper and began to draw out strange plans for their flying machine. Miss Pandemonium got so involved in answering questions that she could not sit back and watch. She was soon down on her hands and knees, helping one of the groups sort out a tricky problem with the rear cog and chain on the bicycle wheel.

Slowly the flying machines began to take shape and the children moved outside to get the rotors fixed. There were some

difficult problems to overcome and there
was glue and tape everywhere. You
couldn't put a foot down anywhere
without treading on something which stuck
to it for the next ten minutes.

Five of the children seemed to have
somehow got themselves completely tied
up with string. It was most strange because
all the knots were right behind their backs
where they could not possibly have
reached for themselves.

'It was Wayne!' cried Amy. 'He did it on purpose.'

'They were no help. They kept getting in the way. I had to tie them up to keep them out of trouble.'

'I think you can release them now,' suggested Miss Pandemonium. 'There, I think we've finished. It's time to put them to the test.'

The bikes made an odd collection. Everyone had found a different way of fixing the rotors above the pilot's head. Some had used thin sticks. Others had used wire rods and string. Now the pilots carefully wheeled their helibikes into the playground, the long rotor blades drooping and bouncing gently as they took up position. The rest of the class watched in silence, wondering if their machines would really fly. Even

Miss Pandemonium was holding her breath.

The pilots climbed on to the saddles. One by one, very slowly and carefully they began to pedal round the playground. The rotor blades circled slowly above their heads, making a low whooshing noise as they sliced the air. The pilots strained over the handlebars to get up speed.

It was hard work pushing those pedals round. They not only drove the rear wheel of the bike but the rotors as well.

'Come on!' cried Miss Pandemonium. 'Pedal faster!' Her words started the rest of the class yelling.

'Faster! Get moving! Come on, Concorde, faster, faster!'

The poor pilots were puffing and panting. Now they stood hard on the pedals. Sshwish, sshwish went the rotors. Round and round went the helibikes.

'Take care!' cried Miss Pandemonium. 'Don't let your rotor blades touch one another.'

There were nine very red faces out on the playground. One helibike was almost up in the air. Its front wheel kept lifting from the ground as if it wanted to take off

but couldn't quite make it. Unfortunately, having one wheel half off the ground made it difficult to steer and very soon one helibike had got too close to another.

The blades met. There was a sharp crack and a large bit of rotor went slicing across the playground and smashed against the school wall. The bikes fell sideways and knocked down another two machines. The other helibikes swerved away violently to avoid the pile-up and smashed head-on into each other. Within seconds the playground had become a major disaster area.

'Oh dear,' murmured Miss Pandemonium, looking anxiously at the pile of wreckage. 'Is everyone all right?'

'Wow!' breathed one of the pilots. 'That was great!'

A loud voice bellowed across the

playground and made everyone (except Miss Pandemonium, of course) freeze on the spot. 'Miss Pandemonium! What on earth is going on out here?'

'We've been making helicopters, Mr Shrapnell.'

'Helicopters? Helicopters! What an utterly ridiculous idea!'

Violet Pandemonium turned and fixed Mr Shrapnell with a pair of innocent grey eyes. 'Oh but, Mr Shrapnell, surely you haven't forgotten? It was *your* idea!'

The Headteacher's jaw dropped open. Once again he was speechless.

4 The Very Friendly Cake

Mrs Bunt no longer felt a twinge of fear when she walked through to the Headmaster's office the next morning. She did not quite know why this was, but she did notice and it sent a little warm glow around her insides. She knew Mr Shrapnell was angry. She realized he might well do one of his volcanic eruptions at any moment, but somehow it no longer worried her. She calmly waited for him to speak, and speak he did.

'It is quite dreadful, Mrs Bunt. Surely you can find someone to replace Miss Pandemonium. She is causing chaos.'

'I shall try, Mr Shrapnell. By the way, how is poor Mr David?'

'I've told you before not to call him
poor. As far as I understand he is lying in
bed with his feet up. He ought to be
ashamed of himself. Now, Mrs Bunt,
would you please get on the telephone and
find someone quiet and sensible instead of
that madwoman in Class Three, before
she has the whole school falling down
round our ears. We must get rid of her as
soon as possible.'

Mrs Bunt had to bite her lips to stop a
smile spreading across her face. 'I shall see
what I can do.'

The sound of a wailing siren came
nearer and nearer. A few moments later
the ambulance careered down the drive
and screeched into the car park. The
driver's door opened and a pile of plastic
tubs, bowls, spoons and knives clattered on
to the tarmac, closely followed by Miss

Pandemonium herself. Her hair looked more like an entire heronry now. She saw Mr Shrapnell watching iron-faced at his window, gave him a massive wave and knocked the wing mirror off the ambulance.

Mr Shrapnell hurried through to the secretary's office. 'Have you got a replacement yet, Mrs Bunt?' The secretary put one hand over the telephone mouthpiece as if she was talking to someone and shook her head.

'Sorry, Mr Shrapnell. Not yet.'

The Head grunted and went back to his office. Mrs Bunt put down the phone and giggled. She had no intention of ringing anyone. She felt that Miss Pandemonium was the best thing that had happened to Dullandon Primary School for ages, and

she was not going to bring it to an end if
she could help it.

'What are we going to do today, miss?'
asked Wayne.

'Help empty my ambulance first of all.
Come on everyone.'

There was a long procession out to the
van to help unload. They found it quite
fascinating. Violet let them all have a go at
making the lights flash and the siren wail.
Then Rebecca tried out the stretcher bed.
Wayne discovered all the bandages and was
all for plastering Rebecca there and then,
but Miss Pandemonium said she felt there
had been enough tying up the day before.

Cheryl picked up some tubs and helped
carry them back to class.

'Miss? Is it true that you want to be an
albatross?'

'Of course. What about you?' But the thought of her teacher as a giant seabird was too much for Cheryl and she couldn't answer.

It took a little while to unload the ambulance and carry all the boxes to the classroom. The children were dying to know what was in the tubs. It wasn't long before they found out.

'We're going to do some cooking today,' announced Miss Pandemonium. It was greeted by groans from a group of children.

'Can't we make our helibikes again?'

'I think we've done enough flying for the time being. It will be a nice change to do some cooking.'

'What are we going to cook?' Caroline asked. 'Can we make ice cream?'

Miss Pandemonium thought for a

second. 'I never thought of that. It would be lovely but I haven't got the stuff with me today. How about making some Friendship Cake?'

'Friendship Cake! What's that?'

'It's something people in Germany used to make, and I think they made it in Canada too. We make a special cake using yeast, flour, sugar, milk and water and we share it with everyone else in the school. That's why it's called Friendship Cake. It's nice to share things with your friends.'

Wayne puzzled over this. 'I shared my black eye with a friend once,' he said.

'How on earth did you do that?' asked Miss Pandemonium.

'Well he gave me a black eye first, so I gave him one back.'

When everyone had stopped laughing,

Miss Pandemonium handed round a large plastic bowl each. Then she put out several bags of flour, bottles of milk, some big stirring spoons and finally a large, creamy brick. The class stared at it.

'What's that?' asked Theresa.

'Yeast. Amazing stuff. It's really alive.'

Luke gave it a poke. 'It's not moving,' he grunted.

'It's not even breathing,' added Karen.

'I think you should take it to the vet, miss,' suggested Rebecca.

'It hasn't got eyes or legs. How can it be alive?'

Miss Pandemonium picked it up and started to break off big lumps to hand round the class. 'Yeast is a sort of fungus and –' She was drowned by a chorus of 'Yuck!' from the whole class. They picked up the yeast, sniffed at it and wrinkled their noses in disgust.

'Oh, it's not that bad,' laughed Miss Pandemonium. 'Every loaf of bread has to start off with some yeast in it. It makes the mixture swell up. Get your bowls and put in some flour.'

It wasn't long before most of the desks, and the floor too, were covered in flour. The children had white smudges on their faces, halfway up their arms, and all over their trousers, skirts and jumpers where they had tried to wipe their hands clean.

John somehow managed to sneeze straight into his bowl, sending a cloud of flour billowing across the classroom.

'Urgh!' cried Sarah. 'Don't eat any of that. John's not making Friendship Cake. He's making a Sneeze Cake!'

'Sarah, do you have to be so revolting?' asked Miss Pandemonium. 'Just mix up your flour, milk and water, like this.'

The class began to stir away. Some took it slowly and carefully. It was obvious that they had stirred things before. Others whisked round at several thousand miles per hour and were surprised to discover half the contents flying out over the sides and splurging across the carpet.

'Oops, sorry,' murmured Amber, as her entire bowl took off from her arm, twizzled about in mid-air and fell to the ground, splattering half a dozen children with soggy flour. But everyone was too busy stirring to take much notice.

'Now for the magic ingredient,' announced Miss Pandemonium. 'In goes the yeast.'

'How much should we put in?' asked Kerry.

'Oh, I don't think it matters. When you've done that add plenty of sugar. The yeast needs sugar to feed on. Now work it all together, cover it with a cloth and we'll put it on the heater to help it work. The yeast likes a bit of warmth to get going.'

Each child brought a large bowl of mixture and it was placed by the

classroom heater. Miss Pandemonium
got some of the children to take bowls to
other classes. After all, she explained, it
was for sharing with other people. Soon
every class in the school had a bowl, or
two or three, of Friendship Cake, much
to their delight and interest.

Miss Pandemonium even sent some
across for Mr Shrapnell and Mrs Bunt.
The Headteacher glared at his and pushed
it to one side of his desk. Mrs Bunt felt
quite honoured.

Back in the classroom there was a strong
smell of yeast and flour. 'Hmmm,' sniffed
Miss Pandemonium. 'Just like a real bakery,
and you are all real bakers,' she added
proudly.

The class grinned back at her, covered
in flour and paste. They got out their
books and began to write about what they

had done, while they waited for the yeast
to take effect.

'She's really nice,' Karen whispered
across to Jackie.

'Shrapnoodle's going to get rid of her,'
Glenn warned darkly. 'Anyhow, she's loopy.
She wants to be an albatross.'

'So what? I want to be an army tank,'
hissed Wayne. 'So just watch it.'

The first sign of success with the mixture
came half an hour later when Mark
noticed the cloth on his bowl bulging
upwards. He took a peek underneath and
was surprised to see that the mixture had
gone all frothy. Little bubbles kept
appearing on the surface and it had risen
to the top of the bowl

'That's what the yeast does!' cried Miss
Pandemonium excitedly. 'It makes the
whole mixture rise.'

'Mine's doing it too!' yelled Julie.

'And mine!'

Right round the class there were yells as they discovered what was happening to their cake. The room was filled with a strong smell of fermenting yeast. Unfortunately the yeast did not stop working once it had reached the top of each bowl. It went bubbling on and on. The truth was that the children had put in far too much yeast, not to mention overdoing the sugar.

The little cloths covering each bowl were rising higher and higher, until you could see the pale, frothing mixture beneath. It looked like a row of bald heads with hankies on top.

Then the bowls started to overflow. The floury paste glooped over the edges and dribbled down to the carpet. There it began to spread, bubbles constantly popping to the surface and releasing the strong gas. The children began to move their desks away from the heater as a slow, smelly tide of flour, milk and water crept towards them.

'Oh dear. I think we may have used too much yeast and sugar,' said Miss Pandemonium quietly.

The same thing was happening in the other classes. The cake was being incredibly friendly and slopping about all over the place. Children were moving out of their classrooms and taking shelter in the hall.

Over in Mr Shrapnell's office, his cake was on the march. It had swept across his desk. Now it was dribbling down all four table legs, carrying several important pieces of paper with it, not to mention five

biros of different colours, a stapler and a
signed photograph of the Education
Minister.

'Mrs Bunt!' he screamed. 'Mrs Bunt!
Have you found a replacement yet?'

'Sorry, Mr Shrapnell,' she shouted back.
'I'm afraid Miss Pandemonium will have
to carry on.'

She watched the Friendship Cake on her
desk carry away the telephone, sat back in
her chair and laughed until the tears
streamed down her face and she had to
hold her sides.

5 Not So Friendly After All

'Don't you worry,' Miss Pandemonium told the Headmaster. 'We have made a bit of a mess but –'

'Bit of a mess!' Mr Shrapnell roared. 'Have you looked down the corridors? There are six tons of porridge creeping round the school. It's everywhere!' He tried to pull his hands away from the sticky goo that covered his desk. It clung to his fingers like chewing gum and pulled into long strands.

'It's not porridge,' Miss Pandemonium pointed out. 'It's Friendship Cake. I was going to say that I do realize we have made a bit of a mess and it is our job to clear it up. Don't you worry, Mr Shrapnell.

We shall soon have the whole building spick and span.'

Mr Shrapnell could hardly refuse this polite offer of help, even though a deep instinct warned him that it would only lead to more trouble. But he felt thoroughly tired and did not know how to argue against this awful woman any longer. Besides, for the moment he was far too busy trying to unstick himself.

Miss Pandemonium carefully made her way back to the classroom, her shoes making loud 'skwuck-skwuck' noises as she waded through the Friendship Cake. The children were all huddled together, feeling very nervous and rather scared by the success of their yeast mixture. It didn't take much imagination to work out what Mr Shrapnell must be thinking.

'Well,' began Miss Pandemonium, 'I

think our Friendship Cake has been a little too friendly. That is entirely my fault and I have explained everything to Mr Shrapnell. There is no need for you to worry.'

Luke whispered hoarsely, 'Will you have to go to prison, miss?' He seemed to think that anyone who upset Mr Shrapnell would end up in jail.

'No, of course not. People don't go to prison for little things like this. However, we've made a mess, so it's our job to clear it up.'

'But that will take weeks!' cried Amber. 'We'll be here for ever!'

'Don't you worry. We shall need plenty of hot water and soap powder. We'll need buckets galore and mops and cloths and the vacuum cleaner. Right then, Cleaning Party – Attention!'

The class stood up straight and waited for orders. One group was sent off for mops, another for buckets and water. Some searched for cloths and soap powder. The last three went off to capture the vacuum cleaner and bring it safely back to base camp. It was a dangerous mission. Wherever those children went they had to overcome the terrible creeping cake that was still slowly spreading through the school.

Then the hard work began. Bucket after bucket of hot water was thrown against the oncoming tide. Soap powder was poured on in a white waterfall. The children seized brooms and mops and scrubbed away in their battle against the flour paste. A thick lather of bubbles began to form. The very large ones broke away and drifted slowly down the corridor or

popped against the walls. The foam grew
and grew until it almost reached from
floor to ceiling.

Cheryl and Caroline gave a shout and
vanished right into the bubble mixture.
They reappeared covered in froth that
glistened with all the colours of the
rainbow and did a little dance. Soon
everyone was doing the same. They
walked up and down showing off to their
friends until suddenly they came face to
face with Mr Shrapnell.

For one second the Headmaster thought

aliens from a distant galaxy must have invaded the school.

He almost turned tail and ran for safety. Then he dimly caught sight of Wayne's round face, masked by sparkling bubbles. 'What is the meaning of this?' he hissed.

'Oh, um, sorry, sir,' trembled Wayne, and as he spoke bubbles came from his mouth and floated away. 'We were just trying to clear up the mess.'

'I suppose this was Miss Pandemonium's idea? I'll get rid of her if it's the last thing I do!' His eyes narrowed to thin, dangerous slits. 'Well, was it? Speak up, boy!'

Wayne was silent. He stared at his feet, not that he could see them beneath a thick layer of foam. He just stared at where he thought they were most likely to be found. Mr Shrapnell gritted his teeth, turned on his heel with a loud 'skwuck!' and went to find Miss Pandemonium.

The children started to breathe again. They looked at each other anxiously. 'Poor old Miss P. She's going to catch it,' murmured Theresa. Peter nodded.

'If she goes . . .' he began, but couldn't finish. The others knew what he meant, but even they could not put into words the despair that was chilling their hearts.

'Come on!' cried Anthony. 'At least we can clear this lot up for her!' He grabbed a mop and went back to work. The rest of the class quickly joined in. It was a team effort against the monster cake, and slowly, bit by bit, they began to push back the tide and gain some ground.

Meanwhile, Mr Shrapnell was fighting his way through the building in his search for Miss Pandemonium, determined to bundle her back into the ridiculous ambulance himself, if necessary, and good riddance. He heard a distant whining noise and set off to investigate, only to walk straight into a ceiling-high mass of froth and foam. He plunged on, half blind, until at last he emerged on the other side, squeaky-clean and smothered in bubbles. Through the froth he saw Violet Pandemonium, vacuum cleaner in hand, trying to suck globs of Friendship Cake from the carpet.

'Miss Pandemonium!' he shrieked. 'What is happening? What are you doing to my beautiful school!'

'Oh, you do look a sight, Mr Shrapnell,' said Miss Pandemonium. 'You're covered in bubbles. Don't you worry though. I shall soon have you nice and clean. We can blow them away with the vacuum cleaner.

You stand quite still now, don't move . . .'

Miss Pandemonium switched the vacuum cleaner on to BLOW. The machine roared, whined, coughed and suddenly spat out huge dollops of Friendship Cake. They blasted through the bubbles and thudded against Mr Shrapnell's chest. He staggered back until he hit a wall, then slowly slipped to the floor.

Miss Pandemonium switched off the vacuum cleaner. 'Oh dear. I think there must have been some cake still stuck down the tube Mr Shrapnell. Sorry about that.' She took a cloth and started to wipe the Headmaster's suit clean. 'There you see, it does come off. Mind you, it's left your jacket a bit streaky. Still, it's nice to be different, isn't it? You know, I think we're actually winning our battle, Mr Shrapnell.'

'Battle?' moaned the Head. 'Battle?' It certainly had been a battle. He'd been battling against Miss Pandemonium from the moment she had first set foot in the school.

'Yes, our battle against the cake. There, you're quite clean again.' Miss Pandemonium gave his nose a quick wipe and polish and helped him to his feet. 'Now, shall we go and see what Class Three have been doing?'

Mr Shrapnell hung back. 'I don't think so, no, I can't take any more of this. I just want to go home and sleep.' But Violet Pandemonium had him firmly by the elbow and was guiding him along the corridor.

A few stray bubbles clung to the walls. There was a strong smell of damp carpet and it squelched underfoot, but the

Friendship Cake had gone. The children had steadily pushed it back until it was right outside the building. That was where Mr Shrapnell and Miss Pandemonium found them. They were pouring bucketloads of water over the last smudge of goo, until it had all trickled away down the drains.

'There we are, all gone. Well done everyone, back to class.'

The children smiled at her and hurried off to the classroom, while Miss Pandemonium walked the Head back to his office. He kept mumbling that he didn't understand anything any longer. Miss Pandemonium called to Mrs Bunt and asked her to make the Head a nice strong cup of tea. 'He's had a bit of a shock,' she pointed out.

Once he was in his office Mr Shrapnell

began to recover. Sitting in his old chair —
now nice and clean, though a touch damp
— his head started to clear. Beyond Miss
Pandemonium he could see the school
timetable, still firmly stuck to the wall. The
school timetable! There was his great
strength. Already he could feel it giving
him new life.

He rose to his feet, pushed past Miss
Pandemonium and ran a keen eye over it.
'I knew it! I knew it, Miss Pandemonium.
It doesn't say anything here about cookery.
Mr David's class is never supposed to cook
at all!'

Violet Pandemonium came over and
glanced at the timetable. Mr Shrapnell
pointed out the whole week of work that
was laid out for Class Three, not to
mention all the other classes in the school.
There was even a timetable for Mr

Shrapnell himself. Miss Pandemonium
carefully read it through.

'Do you see? NO COOKING!'
repeated the Head.

'But how do you manage, Mr
Shrapnell?'

'What? What are you going on about
now?'

'Your timetable here – it must be so
awful for you.' Miss Pandemonium looked
at Mr Shrapnell with a childlike expression
of wonder. 'Your day is quite full up and
you're not allowed one visit to the toilet.
How do you know when to go? And what
about blowing your nose? How do you
manage?'

Mr Shrapnell stared at her. Then he
stared at the timetable. He read his own
timetable again and again. He stared back
at those twinkling grey eyes. Suddenly he

was scrabbling at the wall, tearing down
the beautiful piece of work, scrumpling it
up, shredding it with his bare hands,
smashing it with his fists, throwing it to the
floor, jumping on it and kicking it violently
to all corners of the room.

He stood there, breathing heavily and
staring wild-eyed at Miss Pandemonium.
At last he opened his mouth.

6 Little Things – Big Problems

'Telephone for you, Mr Shrapnell,' called Mrs Bunt. 'I'm putting you through now.'

The Headmaster picked up the receiver and listened. The colour drained from his face. His right eye began to twitch. 'Tomorrow? Tomorrow afternoon? Well, of course, no problem at all. We look forward to seeing you, Mrs Donovan.' He slowly put down the phone. That was it. That must be the last straw. Mrs Donovan was a very important School Inspector, and she was going to visit Dullandon Primary School tomorrow afternoon.

It must mean the end of everything. Mrs Donovan would take one look at Miss Pandemonium and close the entire school.

He'd be sacked, thrown out on his ear after ten years of spotless headship. He walked aimlessly through to Mrs Bunt's office.

'Mrs Bunt? I suppose Miss Pandemonium is here today?'

'Didn't you hear the ambulance, Mr Shrapnell?'

'Yes, yes, though I did try very hard not to. I take it there is no word from Mr David? He won't be in tomorrow?'

'I'm afraid not. The doctor said he mustn't come back to work for at least two weeks.'

Mr Shrapnell nodded brokenly. 'Two weeks,' he muttered. 'Two weeks of Pandemonium.'

'Is there something the matter, Mr Shrapnell?' asked Mrs Bunt.

'No, nothing at all. We only have Mrs

Donovan coming tomorrow afternoon, that's all.'

'Isn't she the Inspector?'

'Yes, the Inspector. The Inspector, Mrs Bunt, but don't let it worry you. I may as well go and stick my head in the gas oven and get it all over with.' He turned away and dragged himself back to his desk. Mrs Bunt watched with interest.

Over in Class Three, Miss Pandemonium had just put an old biscuit tin on her desk.

'What's in there?' asked the class, knowing full well that it could not possibly be biscuits. Miss Pandemonium might carry biscuits in her coat pockets, or at the bottom of her handbag, but never in anything so ordinary as a biscuit tin.

'Mice,' explained Miss Pandemonium. 'You see, my cat is very lazy – he's called

Duvet because he sleeps all day – and he won't catch mice. Unfortunately I've had some mice nibbling away in my kitchen, so I put out some traps for them.'

'Urgh, those aren't dead mice, are they?' muttered Sarah.

'No, I used live traps so I can release them in the wild later. The traps have been out for four nights and when I looked this morning I found I'd caught two wild mice, so I've brought them in to show you. Stuart, I think I saw an old hamster cage out by the sink. See if you can find it.'

Stuart disappeared and a minute later returned with a rather rusty cage. It still had a little exercise wheel inside. Miss Pandemonium opened the top of the cage and took hold of the biscuit tin.

'This is the tricky bit,' she warned. 'Mice are very nervous, so I hope they don't jump out. We don't want them rushing round the class.' She began to prise off the lid, tipping the tin over the cage at the same time. A moment later she gave the tin a shake and two mice slid into the hamster cage. Stuart slammed the lid shut and stood back.

'Well done! That's got them safe and sound.'

'Oh, they're beautiful,' whispered one of the boys.

'Look at that nose,' said Mark. 'It's sniffing. It's all wrinkly.'

'That's because you pong,' Kelly muttered.

'I never knew they were so small,' murmured Jackie.

One of the mice scrambled on to the wheel, which began to squeak and turn. The mouse leaped away as if the wheel had just bitten it. Then it came back, sniffing carefully, and had another go. The children watched, entranced. Miss Pandemonium lifted the cage from her desk.

'I'll put it up here on the shelf where you can all – oh no! Oh dear!'

The cage crashed to the floor as the handle came off in her hands. The door sprang open and the mice were free in an instant. Away they whisked, while half the class threw themselves after them, and the other half stood on their desks yelling.

'They've escaped! They've escaped!'

'It's all right, don't worry,' shouted Miss Pandemonium. 'We'll soon catch them. Where are they now? This way, Kerry! There they are! After them, Amy, quick!'

The mice raced about, twisting and turning as the children tried to close in.

One made a stupendous jump. First it was
on a chair, then running across the
desktops. That caused even more
excitement and the children who were
standing there began to dance about as if
they were on hot coals.

The second mouse found a cupboard
door open and flung itself inside with a
little squeak. Four children plunged in after
it, scrabbling through books and boxes,
rulers, crayons, measuring tapes, puzzles,
everything. All of it came flying out behind

them as they searched madly for one tiny little creature. It was not long before the cupboard was quite bare. Everything lay in a tip behind them.

'There it is, top shelf! Get it!' squealed Sarah. She jumped up, grabbed the shelf, and a moment later the entire cupboard toppled over on them all.

The door banged and Mr Shrapnell strode into the room. He was greeted by a barrage of yells. 'This way! That way! You go round there!'

Before he could speak Miss Pandemonium had seized him. 'You go that way Mr Shrapnell. There's a mouse loose in the class.'

Mr Shrapnell staggered back as a large cupboard heaved itself from the floor and made straight for him. 'What on earth –!'

'Don't worry, that's Glenn and Rebecca,'

explained Miss Pandemonium. 'Quick – I think it went this way. Look there! Up by the books.'

Mr Shrapnell turned just in time to see a little browny-grey lump whizz across several books and disappear behind them. 'Seen it!' he cried triumphantly, and dived after the little beast. Some of the children cheered. Mr Shrapnell began to shuffle the books, searching behind each one. 'I'm sure it's over here somewhere,' he grunted, as Violet joined him.

She caught sight of the mouse crouching behind an atlas, carefully cupped her hands and moved towards it. The mouse was far too quick. It made a flying leap and scampered right up Mr Shrapnell's jacket sleeve. He never noticed a thing. He was still rummaging through the books.

'Oh, Mr Shrapnell,' said Violet. 'I do believe the mouse has gone up your sleeve.'

'Of course it hasn't. I would have felt it.'

'I'm certain it did. I was just about to capture it when it jumped. It went straight up your sleeve.'

Mr Shrapnell stood up. He looked down at his jacket. He held out his arms, but he couldn't see or feel anything. 'It can't have done,' he repeated.

'It did! It did!' shouted Lyndsey and Cheryl.

'Here, take off your jacket,' suggested Miss Pandemonium, already helping him slip it off. She gave the jacket a shake, but no mouse appeared.

'Are you sure about –'

'There it is, under your jumper!' yelled John. A small tell-tale bulge moved along the bottom of one sleeve. Mr Shrapnell

bent his arm, saw the moving lump and
began a frantic mouse-up-the-sleeve dance.

'Argh! It's got me! Out, out, get out you
horrible little beast!'

He shook his sleeve madly and a
moment later the mouse came leaping
out. As luck would have it, the mouse
fell right into the biscuit tin. Wayne was
there with the lid in an instant before
the mouse could recover.

'Well done, Wayne!' cried Mr Shrapnell.

'Three cheers for Mr Shrapnell!' Lee

shouted. 'Mr Shrapnell caught the mouse – and Wayne, of course.'

Mr Shrapnell beamed round at everyone as they cheered. Then the second mouse was spotted cowering down by the blackboard. Mr Shrapnell rolled up his sleeves and put a finger to his lips. A hush fell upon the children. Flushed with his recent success the Headmaster carefully approached the mouse. Bit by bit he got nearer. The mouse ran forward a little way. Mr Shrapnell approached from a different angle. The mouse turned away and ran until it was trapped in a corner.

The class held its breath as Mr Shrapnell pressed forward. Now he was crouching so close he could see every little tiny hair on its back. His right hand began to slide ever so slowly towards the creature. Then, in a flash, his hand shot out, grabbed the mouse, shoved it in the biscuit tin and slammed on the lid.

Class Three let out its breath and cheered. Mr Shrapnell straightened his tie and looked round the room. Miss Pandemonium was standing at the back smiling and clapping. The Headmaster held up one hand and the noise stopped.

'I think there's a bit of mess that needs clearing up in here, children. Miss Pandemonium, would you mind coming to my office for a moment?'

A wave of fear swept across Class Three and they turned to look at their new teacher. They knew what must happen next. They wished there was something they could do to help. They all felt very small and powerless.

Miss Pandemonium gave a bright smile. 'Of course, Mr Shrapnell. I'm just coming.

Make sure you tidy properly, everyone. I shall be back shortly.'

The Headmaster opened the door for her and she passed through. He frowned back at the children and they hastily began work on clearing up the classroom. Then the door shut, and both of them had gone, leaving the children to their worst fears.

'She'll never be back,' Amber said gloomily.

7 An Inspector Calls

'I know what you are going to say, Mr Shrapnell. There are no mice on the timetable.' Miss Pandemonium looked at the Headmaster straight in the eye. He gave her a sharp nod.

'You are quite right, Miss Pandemonium. But you may remember that my timetable was destroyed yesterday afternoon, by myself, after a very, very trying day.'

Violet Pandemonium had to look somewhere else. She found that Mr Shrapnell's expression made her a trifle nervous. He went on.

'There are other copies of the timetable in school of course. However, in the few days that you have been here I have noticed a great deal of excitement among the children. Just forgetting for a moment all the damage and the accidents that have taken place, I have to say that your class has, well – enjoyed themselves. And today, this afternoon . . .' Here Mr Shrapnell took a deep breath, '. . . so did I.'

Mr Shrapnell and Miss Pandemonium gazed at each other. A slow smile came to her face and she gave a little laugh. Mr Shrapnell began to smile too. All at once Miss Pandemonium threw both arms round his neck and planted a plonking kiss on each cheek.

'Oh Mr Shrapnell!' she sighed.

Hastily the Headmaster tried to break away from Miss Pandemonium's giant hug. Just then Mrs Bunt passed by. The school secretary stared at the scene in the Head's office, put a hand to her mouth to stifle a

giggle and ran to her room. Mr Shrapnell
finally managed to break Violet's grip.

'Miss Pandemonium! I'm a married
man.'

'I know that, Mr Shrapnell, but why
shouldn't you hug someone when you're
happy? I always hug people when I'm
happy. Do you know, sometimes I'm by
myself when I'm overcome with joy and I
have to hug a tree or a postbox.'

'I can well believe it,' murmured Mr
Shrapnell. 'But I haven't quite finished yet.
This afternoon I remembered what it is

like to really enjoy being at school. I'm sure Class Three have learned a lot over the last few days, but we do have a big problem to face now. Tomorrow afternoon Mrs Donovan, the School Inspector, is coming here. I'm sure I don't need to tell you what that means.'

'Everybody panic?' suggested Miss Pandemonium brightly.

'Yes. That sums it up quite nicely. I think Mr David's class has swimming tomorrow afternoon – that's if you actually do something from the timetetable for once. Well, not much can go wrong with that, I suppose.'

Violet nodded her agreement. 'Don't you worry, Mr Shrapnell. This will be a show school by tomorrow afternoon. I'm really looking forward to using the swimming pool.' She had gone before the

Head could say anything further. Was it his imagination or had she said that last bit in a funny tone of voice, as if she was planning something?

'By the way,' said Miss Pandemonium, suddenly poking her head round the door, 'you wouldn't like my parrot would you? Norman is ever so nice but he keeps trying to nest in my hair – I don't know why. He's quite tame and can make a noise like an ambulance on red alert. You can have him for nothing.' Mr Shrapnell closed his eyes and gravely shook his head. The last thing he wanted was a parrot that did ambulance impressions. The woman was totally mad.

Class Three were amazed to find Miss Pandemonium back at school the next day. 'How did you escape, miss?' asked Wayne.

Miss Pandemonium laughed and said

she would be teaching them until Mr David was well enough to come back to work.

'Oh good!' they cried. 'What are we going to do today then?'

'Well, we've got swimming this afternoon.' Their faces fell.

'All we ever do is go up and down,' complained Julie. 'We're never allowed to dive in or anything. Can't we do something better, miss?'

Violet Pandemonium gazed at the frowning faces, the begging faces and all the fed-up faces in front of her. She gave a little smile. 'Well, what I would like you to do at the pool is split into four groups and find a way of crossing the pool from one side to the other without getting wet.'

'Without getting wet!' Stuart shouted. 'That's impossible.'

Wayne leaped up. 'No it isn't – you could build a boat.'

'Make a bridge,' suggested Sarah.

'We could throw a rope across and swing from it,' Caroline pointed out. 'Me Tarzan!' she added, beating her chest. 'Come on, Cheeta.' She called to Cheryl. 'Let's get to work.'

By the time morning school was over there were four very different answers to the swimming-pool problem. Group One had decided to build a boat using an old tin tub. They had tried to erect a sail but that hadn't worked very well. Instead they had made some oars out of bits of wood.

Group Two had got the metal PE trestles. They planned to throw a rope from one side of the pool to the other. Then they would hang upside down and swarm across.

The third group had also used PE
equipment and were hoping to build a
bridge using the long planks. The last
group had been very busy all morning
making giant floating shoes out of some
large blocks of polystyrene foam they had
found. The idea was to tie these to their
feet and walk across the water.

As soon as lunch was finished the class
grabbed their costumes and carted all the
equipment over to the pool. Miss
Pandemonium said it would be a good

idea to get changed, just in case. She disappeared into one of the cubicles and came out wearing an old striped Victorian swimsuit. She had tried to put on a cap as well, but there was no way any hat would sit on top of her extraordinary hair.

Each group began preparations. There was a large pile of rope, wood, planks, trestles and a tin tub at one side of the pool. They started to lash bits of wood together and measure out rope. They had almost finished this when Mr Shrapnell appeared at the swimming pool with Mrs Donovan, the School Inspector.

Mrs Donovan was a large, red-faced lady with a loud voice and loud make-up. She stared at the jumble stacked by the pool. Her eyes widened with surprise. She blinked several times and then turned to Mr Shrapnell, who was wishing the

ground would swallow him up. Couldn't
Miss Pandemonium do *anything* right?

'What is going on here?' boomed Mrs
Donovan.

Before he could speak, Miss
Pandemonium explained.

'We're investigating ways of crossing the
pool without getting wet,' she said simply.
The Inspector picked up the plans the

children had drawn and examined some of the equipment.

'How fascinating,' she murmured, and turned to Julie. 'How are you going to cross the rope once it's in position?'

'I'm going to hang upside down,' Julie replied.

'Oh – like a monkey! What a clever idea! I say, this is fun. What about this one. How does it work?'

'You tie these mini-boats to your feet,' Rebecca said, 'and then walk across – I hope.'

'There are so many good ideas,' said Mrs Donovan. She looked seriously at the children. 'I don't suppose I could have a go at one of them? They look so tempting. I'd love to try the boat.'

Rebecca and Peter giggled and said of course she could have a go. Mrs Donovan put down her handbag and began to clamber into the tub.

'Are you going to try one, Mr Shrapnell?' she called across to the Headmaster.

Mr Shrapnell's jaw dropped. Miss Pandemonium gave him a quick nudge and he jerked back to life. 'Oh, yes, yes, but of course. I'm going to be a monkey,' he announced, much to the delight of Wayne's group. Wayne very kindly said that the Headmaster could have first go.

'Thank you very much,' answered Mr Shrapnell, not at all sure that he wanted to be first.

By this time the tin tub was wobbling crazily across the pool and going really well. Mrs Donovan found it a bit difficult to steer but the most important thing was that it worked. 'This is wonderful!' she shouted back to shore, spinning round and round in small circles.

Mr Shrapnell had thrown aside his jacket and was hauling himself on to the rope. It tensed with his weight. This was a real test. He knew that the whole class was watching. He kicked up his legs and locked both feet over the rope. Then he began to pull himself out over the water.

'Go on, sir! Go on!' shouted the boys. 'You can beat her, sir!'

Mr Shrapnell gritted his teeth and hauled even harder. At this point one of the trestles suddenly gave way under the strain. It slid right into the pool and the Headmaster suddenly found himself floundering about in the water.

'Help!' he yelled, rising spluttering to the surface. He thrashed about madly and grabbed the nearest thing in sight, which happened to be the tin tub, still calmly sailing across the pool. Unfortunately, Mr Shrapnell grabbed it so hard the boat completely overturned and threw the School Inspector into the pool.

'Oh!' cried Mrs Donovan with gurgled surprise. 'Oh! It's wet!' as they both sank beneath the surface.

Half of Class Three threw themselves into the pool to rescue the two adults. Miss Pandemonium raced across to the ambulance and switched on the siren and flashing lights. When she got back there were two very bedraggled adults sitting by the pool, with their clothes clinging to them.

'Are you all right?' asked Violet. Mr Shrapnell coughed, spluttered and asked

her to please switch off that awful noise.

The School Inspector wrung out her sleeves and turned to him.

'Mr Shrapnell, I haven't enjoyed a school visit so much for ages. I have to say I am delighted at the change at Dullandon. I used to hate coming here. It was always so stuffy with that wretched timetable of yours. Of course, timetables are useful and necessary, but you can go over the top. As for this class, it is a credit to the school. I can assure you I shall be making a very good report. Now I had better go and get dry somehow.'

Mrs Donovan squelched off to a changing room. Mr Shrapnell watched her go. Then he began to laugh. The children started to laugh. Miss Pandemonium started to laugh. Mr Shrapnell got to his feet and carefully got into the tin tub. He took up an oar.

'May I row you round the pool, Violet?' he asked.

'I'd be delighted, Headmaster,' smiled Miss Pandemonium. She climbed into the tub and they began to paddle sedately round the pool while the children cheered and waved.

And even as the tub began to sink lower and lower with their weight they

didn't care, and slowly slid beneath the
waves, laughing.